JUST A BIT OF FUN

JUST
A BIT OF
FUN

Robert
SWINDELLS

Barrington Stoke

For Big D and Pip:
friends more precious than they know.

First published in 2009 in Great Britain by
Barrington Stoke Ltd
18 Walker Street, Edinburgh, EH3 7LP

www.barringtonstoke.co.uk

This edition first published 2015

Text © 2009 Robert Swindells

The moral right of Robert Swindells to be identified
as the author of this work has been asserted in
accordance with the Copyright, Designs and Patents Act,
1988

A CIP catalogue record for this book is available
from the British Library upon request

ISBN: 978-1-78112-453-6

Printed in China by Leo

Contents

Chapter 1
All Right

I'm Harley. That's my first name, and I bet you can guess my second. Go on – I'll give you three tries and you'll only need one.

Yes that's right – Davidson. Like the bike. My dad called me after a motorbike. Feel free to laugh, by the way. It's all right for you.

People always laugh. I don't care any more. I tell myself it could be worse. I could be called Vespa 50cc or Yamaha 125. That'd be worth laughing at.

I'm a boy, too. That's the other joke people have. They think Harley's a girl's name.

Anyway, I'm in Year 10 at Sorley Hill. It's Thursday afternoon – R.E. with Miss Lake. It's Halloween next week and Miss Lake's dead against Halloween. In the middle of the lesson, she starts slagging it off, same as every year.

"There's our world," Miss Lake says, "and the spirit world. Demons dwell in the spirit world – unclean demons with evil plans who like nothing better than to creep into our world and spread their evil."

She stops and waits a minute or so. She looks at us over her half-moon glasses.

"We're lucky it's not that easy for them to reach us. They need a portal – a door between the worlds. But some of the things we humans do can open up such portals – things like gazing into crystal balls, trying to contact the dead and celebrating Halloween. Halloween is nothing but an excuse to make money. The shops make children think it's all right to do the sorts of things that open deathly portals and let dark forces invade our lives."

Damon Watson's hand goes up. Old Miss Lake looks at him and he goes, "Bit over the top, Miss, don't you think? I mean, come on – Halloween's just a bit of fun, right? Doesn't hurt anyone. It's not like doing smack or putting yourself on the outside of eight or nine vodkas."

It's no good, of course – nothing's going to change Old Lake's mind. She's a fossil. Her brain is set in stone. Every year there's a Halloween disco in the gym, and every year Miss Lake does her best to try and get it stopped. We all have a laugh at what Damon says, but all it does is set Miss Lake off again. The lesson drifts by and we don't learn anything new.

As for me, I can't wait for this year's disco. There's something I've got to do that night.

Chapter 2
Uma Broom

There's this girl, Uma Broom. Daft name, nearly as daft as mine, but Uma's drop-dead gorgeous. She's in Year 11 but I think she fancies me. Well, why not? Anyway, she'll be at the disco, and I'm going as Count Dracula.

Yes, I know. A load of lads'll go as Dracula, they always do. But they'll be nothing like as good as me. None of them, and I'll tell you why.

Last term, our drama teacher got some people from a dance company to come and work with a group of us at school. We had to do different sorts of exercises, mostly working in pairs. Then they got us 'moving to music'. Damon Watson dropped out – said it was lame – but the rest of us got well into it. We stopped feeling embarrassed pretty quick. It wasn't proper ballet – no tights or satin slippers, and we didn't have to pretend to be swans. We wore trackies and trainers, and we did bits out of *Dracula the Ballet*. I bet you didn't know there was a ballet about Dracula, did you? Well, there is, and at the end of the course we danced the best bits of it in front of the whole school.

It was really great. Watson was gutted not to be part of it. I saw the look on his face after the show.

And here's the thing. I was Count Dracula and my costume was fab. It was made just for me by someone from the dance company. I got to keep it, too – because it wouldn't fit anyone else. I even got to keep the black patent shoes that went with it. So when I say I'm going to the disco as Count Dracula, I mean I'm going as Count Dracula, not some sad plonker in a bin bag cloak and a plastic mask from the joke shop.

I was telling you about Uma Broom. The thing about Uma is, she's crazy about nice clothes. Fashion. For lads as well as girls. If you're one of those guys who dresses like his dad, you can forget being seen anywhere with Uma Broom. She wears cool stuff just to take the bin out.

I know that when Uma Broom sees me walking into the gym on Halloween, in my black cloak with the red silk inside and my pointy patent shoes, she'll flip.

And what I say is, bring it on.

Chapter 3
Laugh

Have you got little sisters or brothers?

If you have, you'll know what a pain they can be. I've got one of each. Ryan's ten and Meg's nine. And they're looking forward to Halloween. Course they are.

Ryan and Meg are in primary school, so they don't have a disco. They cut out witches in black paper and pumpkins in orange and stick them on classroom windows. They take pumpkins to school, too. Hollow them out and fix candles inside. Then they bring them home and put them by the door.

And on Halloween night they want to go trick-or-treating, and that's when they start being a pain.

"Harley," Mum goes on Saturday tea time. "Ryan and Meg'll want to go trick-or-treating on Wednesday."

"Uh – yeah," I grunt. I'm trying to catch the footy results on telly. "I know – they always do."

"The thing is, your dad and I aren't happy about kids their age out on the streets after dark."

"So don't let 'em go."

"You always loved trick-or-treating, Harley, and we never stopped you."

"No," I growl. "Dad used to shadow me and my mates like a spy. It was embarrassing."

"It was for your safety," Mum says, "and we want you to do the same for your sister and brother this year."

"Me?" I look at her. "Why me? What's wrong with Dad doing it?"

Mum frowns. "You're 15, Harley. It's time you started to help out with the little ones.

They're to go to the houses on Park Villas, nowhere else. And you'll have them home by 8 o'clock sharp."

"But, Mum, it's the disco that night," I say. "It kicks off at seven. If I have the kids till eight I'm gonna miss half of it."

"What time does it finish?" says Mum.

"Ten."

"Well, if you get into your outfit before you take the kids out, you'll be at the disco by 8.20. That gives you more than 90 minutes to dance, eat, do whatever. That's plenty of time."

I've missed all the footy results now. I shake my head. "No way am I doing it, Mum."

Mum looks at me. "Let's see what your father has to say about it when he gets in, shall we?"

I snort. I know what Dad'll have to say. What he'll say is, "When you're working, bringing money into the house, you can please yourself. Until that day comes, you'll do as you're told and like it."

Well, no, I won't like it. He can make me do stuff, but he can't make me like it.

But what can I do? I can't believe I'll be missing the disco. Maybe Ryan and Meg will take a bribe? They're in Meg's room, playing computer games. I knock and enter.

"Hey, kids," I say.

"Get out, Harley," Ryan snarls. "Can't you see we're busy?"

"Listen," I say. "It's Bonfire Night in under two weeks. Got plenty of money for fireworks, have you?"

Meg shakes her head. "No, but it's Halloween first. When we're out trick-or-treating, some people will give us money as their treat. And we can give that to Dad to buy fireworks."

"Dream on," I say. "Most people don't give money. Most people give sweeties and stuff. I'll give you three quid each for fireworks, if ..."

"If what?" Meg asks. I can see she doesn't trust me.

"If you stay in on Wednesday instead of trick-or-treating."

Ryan twists round on his chair. "Stay in on Halloween?" he says. "You're having a laugh, aren't you?"

I stay cool. "No, I'm serious. Three quid. Each. You won't get that knocking on doors."

"We'll take the chance," he says. "Shut the door when you leave, big bro."

What can you do?

Chapter 4

Toffee

One thing you can do is up your offer.

Which is what I try on Sunday morning. "Four," I hiss across the breakfast table. Mum's gone out to wash the car. Dad's in the garden. "Four quid each, how about it?"

"Pathetic, Harley," Ryan says. "One rocket costs three quid. We'd get, like, two fireworks each for missing Halloween. That's rubbish."

"Five," I say. "Final offer."

"Stuff it," my sweet little sister snarls.

So I know I've got no hope.

So here we are, the three of us, 7 o'clock Wednesday, dolled up and ready to go.

Dad's giving me the eye. He's like, "Think on, Harley. Park Villas only. They're not to step off the pavement, let alone cross the road. And don't let them out of your sight, not for a second. If anyone invites them indoors, you go in with them. You never know what goes on in other people's houses."

This is totally over the top. Park Villas is all piano teachers and other old people. How would they harm anyone? They're too busy saving the whales. But it's no use arguing. "It'll be fine, Dad," I say. "Let's go, monsters."

We set off. It's a damp, misty evening. Ryan's dressed up as a skeleton. He's got a black suit with greenish glow-in-the-dark bones on it and a hood. Meg's a witch in rags and a pointy hat. Her eyes glitter as she peeps through the holes in her stiff green mask. She's excited.

"You both look stupid," I tell them. What I want is to be at the disco with Uma Broom. So why should I be nice? If any of my mates clock me baby-sitting I'll have to kill myself.

There's only one side to Park Villas. It's a long line of gloomy old houses. The bay windows look out over Jenner Park. No one can build there because rich Mr Jenner – who was an inventor or something – left it to the people of Sorley.

We stop at number 1. There's no gate, just a short, damp path and two steps up to the door.

"Go on, then," I say. "What're you waiting for?"

Meg shivers. "Dunno, Harley. It's always scary, the first one."

"Yeah, well." I shrug. "They do say the woman who lives here is mad."

"Mad?" Meg gulps.

"As a hatter. She used to teach music, but she murdered a pupil and hid the body inside the piano. The blind man who came to tune the piano found it."

"Oooh!" Meg shudders. "I'm not knocking here, then."

"Don't be such a wimp," Ryan says. "Can't you see Harley's just trying to spoil it for us? He didn't want to bring us out."

I try my Count Dracula voice. "Go right ahead, young sir – the lady and I will follow you."

He goes up the path first, I'll give him that. Of course, I've made it all up. I know that an old guy lives here by himself. Meg hangs back till she sees the old man open the door. I lurk behind the hedge so no one sees me. What sort of loser goes trick-or-treating when they're 15, for God's sake?"

The old guy's really into it. He cries out when he sees Meg and Ryan, then shakes with fake fear as he backs along the hall to get them a treat. Never grow up, some people. I turn my back and stare across the road at the jungle of trees by the park wall.

And that's when I first see the white thing, fluttering. It's half hidden among the trees, so I can't see it very well. Could be a plastic bag, I tell myself, stuck on a branch, flapping in the wind.

What wind? There's isn't any wind. It wouldn't be misty if there was. But the white bag is fluttering about in the trees. Something's making it move. Or maybe it's a barn owl – I think they're white. Doesn't look much like a barn owl. More like a flag. A raggy white flag.

"Wake up, Harley!" It's Ryan, but I damn near jump out of my skin. "What's up?" he says.

"N ... nothing." I shake my head. "It's nothing. What did you get?"

"All these." He opens the bag on his belt. It's crammed with toffees. "Meg's got just as many."

"Huh!" I grunt. "You can't buy fireworks with toffees, can you?"

"Plenty more houses," Meg says. "Come on."

I look across the road again, quickly. I can't see anything white. I trot after the toffee monsters.

Chapter 5
A Trick

"Trick or treat?"

"I'll trick or treat you, you little monkeys. Clear off before I let the dog out."

We're at number 2. The kids are – I'm waiting by the gate. Number 2 does have a gate. When the woman starts yelling, I shove it open and walk up her path.

"That's my brother and sister you're bawling at, you sad old cow," I snarl. She looks at me like I'm something the cat sicked up.

"Get out of my garden this instant, and take your brother and sister with you, or I'll call the police."

"You must be one of those sad oldies who were never young themselves," I hiss in her face. She steps back, slams the door in mine. "Come on, kids," I snap. "Idiots like her aren't worth bothering with."

"At least she didn't set the dog on us," says Meg as we get back to the street.

"I bet she hasn't even got a dog," says Ryan. "Why don't we dream up a really bad trick to play on her."

"No way!" I grab their hands and we walk away. "Like I said, she's not worth the bother. Better luck at number 3, eh?"

Meg peers up the path. "Come with us, Harley," she whispers.

I shake my head. "No, but I'll tell you what – my offer's still open. You can take that four quid each and I'll get you home safe right now if you want."

"It was five quid," Ryan snaps, "and you can keep it. C'mon, Meg." He takes her hand and they set off down the next garden. This one's full of big bushes. I sit on the low wall to wait.

It's there again, just opposite. Fluttering. We've moved, and the thing's moved with us. Weird. I look hard into the mist but I can't make out what it is.

I hear the kids knock and the door open. "Trick or treat," Ryan says. No one yells, so that's all right. I get up, walk to the pavement edge, peer across.

It isn't a flag – it's not the right shape. It doesn't have a proper shape. It's like someone's waving a bit of white silk in the air, making swirly patterns. Except no one's there. The thing's moving all by itself, in the black under the trees.

This time when we move on, I keep my head turned to the right so I can watch it. I tell myself it can't really have followed us. It must be my eyes or a trick of the light – an optical illusion. But I don't feel like turning my back on it.

"We got a pound each," Ryan crows. "Soon beat your stupid fiver now, Harley."

"Right," I say. "Good." I'm not really listening to him. We're at the gate to number 4, and the thing's still level with us. "Go on, then," I croak. "Off you pop." I can't let the kids see I'm scared, cos I'm not. I just want to know what the thing is, that's all.

Meg and Ryan go off up the path, all giggles. They're having fun now, not nervous at all. Well, they've got their big brother backing them up, haven't they? They don't know their back-up's getting spooked by a rag on a twig.

I stand and stare across at the trees, at the park, at the white thing. A car swishes past. Did the driver notice it? Even if he did, it'd be no big deal. It's a torn bag, for God's sake.

"You're a bit of litter," I say. "That's all you are."

Am I going mad – talking to litter?

"Hello, Harley, we're done here." I turn and stick a grin on my face. Meg's grinning too. "More money," she tells me. "Best Halloween ever."

I nod. "That's good, Meg. You two carry on to number 5. I'll be with you in a sec."

Ryan stares at me through his skull hood. "Is something wrong, Harley?"

"No, no." I shake my head. "Everything's cool, Ryan. I'm crossing the road for a minute, that's all. Don't follow or you'll get me in trouble. Do number 5, wait for me outside 6, OK?"

Ryan shrugs. "Right, Dracula," he says. "Come on, Meg."

I don't want to cross. Don't want to be any closer to that thing than I am now, but that's stupid. I'm letting my fear make a prat out of me. Because that's all it is – fear. I'm going to show it who's boss. No one makes a prat out of me.

A truck's coming. I let it pass, hope the white thing vanishes after the truck's gone. It doesn't. I start to cross the road, my eyes fixed every second on that scrap of white. As I get to the other side, something shifts in my head and what I see now is different. It's like when you stare at that trick picture and it stops being two black faces and turns into a white vase.

The white plastic bag's gone. Now I can see a girl standing among the trees. A girl in a white dress. I don't know why I didn't see her before.

The moon breaks through and pours soft light on the girl's face and my heart kicks me in the ribs. The girl is Uma Broom. And she's smiling at me.

Chapter 6
Undead

"Uma, hey!" I yell. My heart's thumping. "Why are you … I mean, what are you doing here, what about the disco?"

I've lost it totally. I'm talking rubbish. It's the shock. It doesn't make sense. Why is Uma here?

Uma says nothing, just stands there smiling. Maybe she missed me at the disco, came looking for me. But that's crap. A girl like Uma can have any guy she wants. Why would she leave the disco for me? And anyway, how did she know where I was?

A horrible thought makes me go hot all over. She's come for a laugh. Somehow, she found out I was baby-sitting in my Count Dracula kit, and she's here to mock. There's maybe half the kids in my year behind those trees, peeing themselves laughing.

"Come for a giggle, have you, Uma?" I say. "You and the others? Well, go on then – laugh. See if I care."

I do care, but no way am I going to let Uma see that. I'm turning away and she laughs, but it isn't a mocking laugh. It's the sing-song laugh she uses with her friends – the laugh that melts my bones when I hear it at school. I've got to do something, so I swing myself over the wall. If Uma Broom wants me to join her in Jenner Park, I'm not complaining.

I get up close to her, can't believe my luck. When I can nearly reach out and touch her, she turns and runs off between the trees, still laughing. Something tells me she's not running to get away from me, but to tease.

"Here I come," I shout, "ready or not." If Uma wants to play chase, that's OK with me. In fact, it's a great idea.

She's out of the trees now and she jogs onto the footy field. The white dress soaks up moonlight. She has on these little silver shoes. They must be all messed up with mud and wet grass. She's still laughing, like little bells ringing.

I run fast across the grass. I need to catch her and ask her what she's playing at, but I seem to be getting no closer. "Uma!" I gasp. I feel like a fool. "Hang on a minute, I want to tell you something."

She looks back and slows down a bit. The gap between us gets smaller. The pond's just in front of her, she'll have to stop now.

"Uma," I gasp again. "We're missing the disco. How about if you and me ...?"

The words die away as I say them. Uma's at the pond, but she doesn't stop. The moon has made a silvery path across the water. Without stopping for a second, she's on it. I croak a warning but there's no splash. She jogs out across the bright surface of the pond, and now her laughter mocks me as I stand frozen and watching.

Some guy wrote graffiti on the toilet wall at school – "Uma Broom walks on water." But that's just what guys say about someone who's cool. No one really walks on water. No one. And yet ...

You've got to believe what you see, haven't you? And there's Uma, out in the middle of the pond, dancing and laughing, swirling that beautiful dress.

As I stare with my mouth open, some words of Miss Lake's come back to me – "Unclean demons with evil plans ..."

"It isn't HER, you plonker!" screeches a voice inside my skull. "That's not Uma Broom. It isn't a person at all. It's a ..."

Yes, I know how daft it sounds, and I know exactly what you're thinking. You're thinking, 'He's flipped his lid, fallen out of his tree. He'll be telling us next she got on her broomstick and flew away. He'll say that's why she's called Broom.'

Well, you can think what you like – you weren't there. I was, and I know what I saw.

I stand and watch her – or it or whatever – dancing on the top of the pond. It's for real – right in front of my eyes, and I'm so busy staring that it takes a minute or two before I remember what I'm meant to be doing.

The kids – I'm meant to be looking after the kids. "Don't let them out of your sight," said Dad. "Not even for a second."

And where are they now? Miles away from me. I wouldn't hear if they shouted, or know if they got run over by a truck.

I've let this girl – this thing that looks like a girl – take me away from my brother and sister. And there's me saying, "No one makes a prat out of me." Well, she has, hasn't she? And that's nothing to what Dad'll make out of me if anything's happened to the kids.

The thought of Dad when he's angry scares me into looking away from that weird dance on the water, or I swear I'd still be standing there.

As it is, I start running back across the footy field – I don't even look back. Thinking about what I'd see if I did look back makes me run even faster. I sprint back to Park Villas and I'm fretting all the way.

How long have I been in the park? Five minutes? Ten? I haven't a clue, it's as if time

stopped the second I saw Uma – if it was Uma.
That thing took over my brain, drove out
everything else. Now I feel as if I'm in a dream
as I fly gasping over the muddy turf.

Then I'm under the trees. I can see the
street-lamps, the road. "Why?" screams a voice
in my head. Why did that thing lead me away?
What did it want with me? Deep down I know,
of course I do. It was one of Miss Lake's demons,
and it led me off so that its mates could get a
crack at Meg and Ryan.

Twigs and branches pluck and rip at my
clothes, but I don't care. I get over the wall
and scan the houses. No one's waiting outside
number 6, or 7, or 8. Cold fear floods my guts.
I dash across the road without looking. If
anything's coming I'm dead, but I don't care. I
blunder up the path of number 5 and hammer on
the door.

"Come ON!" I yell. "Are you all flipping deaf
or what?"

I'm about to give the door a kick when it
cracks open. A guy in glasses blinks through the
gap. He looks like an owl in a hollow tree.

"What's your problem, Dracula?" he asks. "Don't you think you're a bit too old to be trick-or-treating? A bit ... er ... undead?"

Chapter 7

Dog

"I ... I'm not trick-or-treating," I blurt out. "I've lost two kids. Did they knock here?"

He nods, calm. "A witch and a skeleton. We gave them a pound or two and they left."

"How long?" I ask.

"Huh?"

"How long ago?" I ask again.

"About ten minutes. I heard them knock next door."

"Number 6, yeah?"

"Yes. Mr and Mrs White. They're all right."

I nod. "Thanks, I'll try there."

"Good luck. Call back if there's anything I can do."

They're not at number 6 now, unless they're inside. I ring the bell. I see a light go on somewhere. I'm like, "Come on, for God's sake." I hop from foot to foot and look across at the black trees in the park.

A woman opens the door.

"Two kids," I say, all out of breath. "Are they here?"

"Kids? You mean the trick-or-treaters?" She shakes her head. "They ran away before I'd a chance to give them their treat. We'd never invite children in anyway."

"They ran?" I don't understand.

"Yes," the woman says.

"Which way?" I ask.

"I don't know, dear. I didn't watch them go. Are they missing?"

"They just seem to have ... vanished," I say.

"I'm so sorry. You can come in and use the phone if you need to."

"The phone?" I don't see how that would help.

"Yes, to call the police," the woman tells me.

"Oh, no, that's fine, I've got my mobile. I hope I don't have to ring the police."

The woman smiles. "Oh, of course." She frowns. "Do the children have a mobile with them?"

I shake my head. "Not tonight – but thanks." I turn and hurry down the path.

"Children almost always turn up safe and sound, you know," she calls after me.

"Almost" is a dangerous word.

I look down Park Villas. A black cat is sniffing at the foot of a street-lamp. A car speeds by, music thudding out. Across the road, way down, an old man is walking his dog in the shadows of the trees.

'I don't half wish I was you,' I think, 'or the guy in that car.' Someone who hasn't lost kids, who doesn't know that there's something dancing and laughing out there in the park tonight. 'In fact,' I think, 'I'd rather be your dog than me.'

At least if I was a dog I wouldn't have to face Mum and Dad.

My brain's shut down. I'm in a sort of dream, doing nothing but gawp. I haven't a clue how long I stand gazing down the road, but I'm jerked out of it by a crash of splintering glass. Then there's a scream, then wild laughter. Children's laughter.

It's coming from number 2. What was it Ryan said – "Why don't we dream up a really bad trick to play on her?"

"No!" I yell. "For God's sake, no. Ryan! Meg!" I pelt back to number 2, shouting like a madman.

The gate's open. I brake, swerve through the gate, dash up the path and stop dead. It's worse than I expected – much worse.

The middle window is smashed. There's a drift of glittering bits of glass on the sill, and sharp glass teeth jut out of the window frame. The front door is open. The woman is standing on the step, her arms up in front of her face.

Dark, sticky stuff is smeared all over her hands, knees and hair.

Meg and Ryan have got their backs to me and they're throwing handfuls of small stones at her and chanting, "Where's your dog? Where's your dog? Where's your dog?"

Everything happens at once. Fast foot-steps behind me and someone gasps, "My God, oh my God!" A guy with white hair grabs my sleeve. He's the man who lives at number 3. "Miss Conrad," he says. "What on earth are you doing to Miss Conrad?"

Before I can reply another guy comes up the path. "I heard glass," he says. "Is something the matter?" He's the old man from number 1. He peers at what's going on in the garden and gasps. "They're murdering her!" he cries. "Stop them, someone call the police."

Both men turn on me. "You put them up to this, you must have. Stop them right now, or we will." They look nasty. They're angry and their faces look mean. I dash up to the door.

"Meg, Ryan," I shout as I grab them, "what the hell d'you think you're doing?" I swing them round, shake them as hard as I can. "Can't you

34

see you're killing the lady? What's wrong with you?"

Meg pushes her face up to mine. She looks totally different. Her face is so twisted. I feel as if don't know my sister at all.

"Why do you care, Harley?" she snarls through her teeth. "You said she's not worth bothering with, so let go of me before I rip your face off."

Meg's taken her mask off but her eyes are empty and ugly. I jerk my head away from her but not fast enough. A hand flashes out and claws like hooks rip into my cheek. It hurts. I let go of Meg as I clap my hand to my face. She skips away from me and spits like a cat. And I know with a cold shock that it isn't Meg at all.

Ryan twists free too. He joins his sister on the lawn. The chanting starts again.

"Where's your dog? Where's your dog? Where's your dog?" They point their fingers at Miss Conrad and mock her. They stab the air in time with their chant.

All this time, Miss Conrad's trying to get back in the house. Her hand is feeling for the door but she daren't take her eyes off the kids. I move up to the door so I'm standing between her and them. There's a really bad smell – the stuff on her is dog shit. There's more on the step, on the door handle and the letter box. I reach out. What I want to do is help her back inside.

"Don't touch me!" Miss Conrad shouts and jerks her arm away. "Don't you dare lay hands on me." She starts to back towards the open door. "What sort of people are you? Look what the children have done to me and my house."

I look at her and then back at Meg and Ryan. I shake my head. "I ... I don't think it's children we're dealing with," I manage to say.

"Don't think it's children we're dealing with," Ryan chants in a silly voice.

"Children we're dealing with," Meg screeches.

The two of them burst into laughter and skip round the lawn.

Chapter 8
Aliens

Miss Conrad shakes with fear and anger. "This is too much. I'm ringing the police right now," she splutters.

The man who lives at number 1 has come up to the door. "Yes – we need the police here right now," he growls. "Assault and battery, criminal damage – this is a police matter, all right." He grabs my arm. He's not strong, and he's so old that I could knock him down easily. But I don't. I so don't want the police involved.

It's then that I see the other guy has his mobile out. 'Does he have footage of the kids?' I think. Of me, of the damage? Evidence. Now he's calling a number on the phone. "What are you doing?" I shout out to him.

"What d'you think I'm doing?" he yells. "Calling the police, of course!"

"No, wait," I beg. "Please. We're not really like this, I promise. We live just round the corner on Grasmere Drive. The kids have never been in trouble, and neither have I. Our dad's the boss of security down at the shopping centre. He might lose his job if ..."

The woman glares at me. "Your sister and brother should have thought of that before they smashed my window, smeared dog dirt everywhere. Before they threw stones at me to kill me."

I shake my head. "Not to kill you," I say. I'm so scared I say the first thing that comes into my head. "They're little, they don't understand, they only meant to play a trick on you ..."

"A trick?" She looks down at herself and at her filthy hands, then over at the smashed window. "You call this a trick? It isn't a trick, it's a wicked assault. People don't deserve to be attacked in their own homes like this. It's totally wrong."

I nod. I'm scared witless, but I see that the old man from number 3 is listening. He hasn't made his call yet.

"I know," I tell her. "You're right, but you see …" I stop and take a deep breath. "This is going to sound daft, but I think something's taken them over."

"What – like aliens, you mean?" The woman glowers at me. "You've the nerve to stand there and tell me that pair of little monsters are aliens from … from where – Mars?"

I shake my head. "No – no, not aliens. It's Halloween, you see. Our R.E. teacher reckons that at Halloween things – portals – open up between the spirit world and this one, and demons come into our world. I didn't believe her, but now …"

I nod at Ryan and Meg, who are standing still and silent on the lawn. "Now, I think it could be true, because I've never seen my brother and sister act like this. In fact, they don't even look like my brother and sister. Their eyes …"

"This is all rubbish," says the man from number 3. "Let's stop messing about and get the police here." He looks at me. "Try telling the cops these kids have demons in them, see where it gets you."

"Wait, please, Arthur." Miss Conrad holds up a hand. The man from number 3 sighs and puts his phone away. She looks at me. "Where do you go to school, young man?"

"Sorley Hill."

"Your R.E. teacher must be Mildred Lake, then?"

"Yes, that's right." I feel a flicker of hope. "D'you know her?"

The woman nods. "We were at college together." She looks towards the lawn where Meg and Ryan, silent now, stand watching us. "She talks a lot of sense, does Mildred Lake. Always did." She shivers. "And she might well be right about 'demons'. I've never liked Halloween, and I don't like trick-or-treating either."

"Well, I've always loved it," I tell her, "but I'm not so sure now. Listen, I promise I'll clean everything up, and I know my dad'll pay for the window, only please don't get the police."

The woman isn't sure. "Well, I don't know …" She shows me her hands, points with a foot at the filthy step. "All this. My window. It's all most upsetting. The mocking, the stones. I shouldn't have to …"

"I know, you're right." I take out my phone. "Look, I'm phoning my dad. He'll be horrified when I tell him what's happened and he'll come right away. We're not vandals, Miss Conrad."

Miss Conrad doesn't seem sure. I wait.

I hope the two old men will give me a chance – that they won't ring the police for her. I'm looking at the kids as well – one more taunt, one more chant, and we're stuffed.

We all stand silent and wait for Miss Conrad to tell us what she's going to do.

This silence goes on for a long time. I picture what would happen if the police call at our place and tell Dad his kids have attacked an old woman with stones and smashed up her house. He'll love that, and he'll admire the hell out of me for the great job I've done looking after the kids.

Not.

After about six million years, Miss Conrad speaks.

"Phone your father if you wish," she says, "but I don't want anyone to see me like this. He must come tomorrow if he wishes to talk to me."

She turns to her two neighbours. "Thank you, Arthur and Neil, for coming to my rescue. My attackers might have been grown men, not children, in which case you'd have been in some danger yourselves. I'm grateful to you both." She doesn't look at me or the kids, but goes in and closes the door.

The old men look at me and then at each other. Arthur's like, "You're luckier than you deserve, lad. You can thank your lucky stars our Miss Conrad was at college with your Miss Lake, because that's what swung it."

I watch the pair shuffle away down Miss Conrad's path, then I walk over to the kids. Their eyes look normal now. That awful emptiness has gone.

"Ryan, Meg, I'm phoning home," I tell them. "I don't know what got into you both while I was gone, but it's my fault. I should never have left you. Are you feeling all right now?"

They nod. They both look worn out. "I don't know what it was either, Harley," Meg says, her voice quiet. "But I felt it go from me. It was when Miss Conrad said that Miss Lake might be right about demons. It was as if something flew out of me. It had been found out, you see, so it flew away." She frowns. "Does that make sense?"

I nod. "Perfect sense, Meg. Maybe it thought we'd fetch someone to get rid of it – you know, cast it out? Maybe it hurts, being cast out."

Ryan's staring at the smashed window. "We wouldn't dare do stuff like that," he says, "but we did, didn't we, Harley?"

"You did, Ryan, sort of, but it wasn't really you." I look at him. "Did you feel something fly away from you too?"

He frowns. "Maybe, I don't know," he says. "I felt scared and ... angry, I think."

"That was it, Ryan – the demon," I tell him. "The demon was scared and angry, not you. So it flew away."

"I ... picked up dog poo," whispers Meg, "with my hands." She's rubbing them on her witch's skirt. "They stink. I think I'm going to be sick."

And then she throws up in the middle of Miss Conrad's lawn.

I call home, tell Dad there's been a bit of trouble, say he'd better come and look. He's there straight away. Mum's with him.

I won't bang on about it. He is horrified. They both are. Dad fetches cloths and cleaning stuff from the car. I help him clean up Miss Conrad's door and letter box. It's dark but we do our best to clean the step too.

Dad writes a note and puts it through the letter box.

Dear Miss Conrad

We're so, so sorry. I'll be back in the morning to set things right. I'll have my cheque-book with me. Thanks for taking it so well.

Tom Davidson

By this time Meg and Ryan are in floods of tears. The shock's gone and the full horror of what's happened is sinking in. To tell you the truth, I'm not feeling too great myself. We pile into the car and Dad drives us home.

There's still half an hour of the disco left to go, but my outfit's a mess. And, anyway, me and Halloween are finished.

I go to bed the same as Ryan and Meg, but I can't sleep.

Chapter 9
Stuff

Next morning, it's the first of November. The stuff that happened last night seems like a dream to me. I think Ryan and Meg feel the same.

But it wasn't a dream. Dad's already at Park Villas. He's kept his promise to Miss Conrad. I can tell that Mum's bursting to ask the kids about it all, but she doesn't. She lets them miss school. They're still worn out and very upset.

I've said it was all my fault. "I saw something," I say. "Under the trees in the park. It drew me away. I forgot all about Ryan and

Meg. Something got to them while I was gone. I'm really sorry."

I mean it.

But I do have to go to school.

"You must be dying to know how the disco went," Mum says. "And your friends will really want to know what happened to you."

Yeah, right. Like I'm gonna tell them I spent Halloween baby-sitting. How uncool is that? Mums just don't get it.

I get to school at 8.30. First guy I see is Damon Watson. "Davidson!" he yells, so everyone can hear. "Where were you last night, dude? You missed the best disco ever."

I shrug. "Not bothered, Watson."

He looks at me. "Not bothered? I thought you couldn't wait to swagger into the gym in your Dracula kit."

I pull a face. "Well, yeah – I have to admit I was looking forward to running it by Uma Broom, see if it'd make her fancy me."

Watson shakes his head. "Wouldn't have happened anyway, mate – she didn't show up either."

Weird, or what?

And no. It can't have been her in the park – I'm not saying that. But stuff happens, doesn't it, sometimes? Stuff we can't explain.

Two things I do know. One – Miss Lake's not the sad old fossil I took her for. And two – I go cold every time I hear that sing-song laugh I first heard in Jenner Park on Halloween.

Our books are tested
for children and young people by
children and young people.

Thanks to everyone who consulted on
a manuscript for their time and effort in
helping us to make our books better
for our readers.

About the Author

ROBERT SWINDELLS was born in Bradford in Yorkshire. He wasn't clever at school, but he was good at making up stories and he won his first writing competition at the age of 14.

Robert left school at 15 and had lots of different jobs before he trained as a primary school teacher. After several years of teaching, he became a full-time writer.

Robert has a Master's degree in Peace Studies and was sent to jail for seven days for helping blockade Whitehall as a member of the anti-nuclear movement.

Robert has written 70 books for young people and has won the Carnegie Medal, the Children's Book Award (twice), the Angus Book Award, the Other Award, and the Sheffield Children's Book Award.

He lives with his wife on the Yorkshire moors.

Also by **Robert Swindells** ...

It was my birthday really, but it could have been
my deathday. It very nearly was in fact.

Alfie has a great new SLR and he can't wait to
try it out. But while he snaps artistic shots of the
street outside his home, a gang of robbers smash
the window of a jewellery shop and make off with
loads of watches and rings.

Alfie's got the whole thing on camera. Now a lot
of people want to get their hands on his SLR. And
they will stop at nothing ...

BURN OUT

Feel the heat ...

Robert
SWINDELLS

From the Carnegie Medal-Winning author

All his life, Josh has felt like a loser. But
then he joins Nick Mitchell's gang, and sets fire
to his first car. And that blaze lights a spark
somewhere in Josh's soul.

But flames spread, and soon Josh's whole life
is under threat ...